The Third Day

Book One

BEN RICARDO

The Third Day
Copyright © 2022 by Ben Ricardo

ISBN
978-1-957378-82-4 (Paperback)
978-1-957378-81-7 (eBook)

Table of Contents

chapter

1

L ewin thought sex would be this perfect moment where all the things he went through being closeted and then coming out repeatedly would be worth it once he finally had sex. Or that it'd at least be fun.

It's not quite how it works out.

He finishes with the guy and collects his clothes, getting out as quickly as possible. They'd been dancing around each other for most of the night, and he can see out of the bathroom window that the sun is rising as he pulls his socks back on. Compulsively, he turns on the cold tap, cups his hands under it, and rinses his mouth three, four times, but can still taste the guy's tongue in his mouth. He looks contemplatively at the toothbrushes next to the mirror and wonders how low he wants to go in the name of surviving casual sex tonight but decides that's too far. So instead, he rinses his mouth again with a little toothpaste to help.

It doesn't.

The guy is sitting at his kitchen table with - presumably - a roommate as Lewin exits, and he offers Lewin a casual wave and asks, "Hey, got places to be?"

Lewin forces a grin, shrugging as he says, "Don't want to draw out the awkward morning after any longer than absolutely necessary." The roommate reacts the way an average person would to that level of social incompetence, eyes widening slightly and trying to get the guy's attention to laugh at Lewin with him. Still, the guy just breaks into laughter with Lewin as though he's charmed.

Lewin sees his jacket is on the back of the guy's chair and considers forgetting it for a second. That option is taken from him as soon as he thinks it, though because the guy is out of his chair and bringing it over to him.

"Oh, thanks," Lewin says, reaching for it, but the guy holds it up like he wants Lewin to step into it. On autopilot, Lewin does. He shivers at the feeling of hands smoothing the arms of his jacket down, one coming to rest at the small of Lewin's back as he's gently led towards the door.

Creep, Lewin thinks. He doesn't all the way mean it. The hand is big, spanning a lot of his lower back, and a big part of Lewin likes it; likes how possessive it feels. Another part isn't going to feel steady until he's had a shower.

Once they're out of the kitchen and standing in the partly open apartment doorway, the guy drops his hand from Lewin's back only to pull him in by the lapel of his jacket, stopping just short of kissing him. His hand lands on Lewin's jaw and he thumbs at Lewin's bottom lip.

Lewin's stomach has bottomed out. He also can't take his eyes off the guys' mouth because he looks like a Ken doll and his lips are actual sin to look at. He'd been an incredible kisser, too. Lewin doesn't know what's wrong with him.

"Can I…?" the guy asks, using his thumb to part Lewin's lips just enough so Lewin can't stop the embarrassing squeak that comes out, and he finally thinks, *oh, fuck it*, and leans forward to press his lips to this guy's perfect ones again. He makes a soft, approving sound into Lewin's mouth, but they seem to be on the same page on one thing, at least, because their kiss stays fairly chaste.

Another minute passes before Lewin reminds himself of the feel of his guy's tongue in his mouth and breaks off the kiss, maybe too suddenly to be casual. The guy's eyes open. He seems a little surprised, but a smile spreads across his lips as he cups Lewin's face in both his hands and pulls him in for one quick, chaste press of lips. Then, he pulls back, resting his arms on Lewin's shoulders, so they're still standing close. So there's no polite way to pull away.

Lewin suddenly can't meet his eyes, clearing his throat.

"Hey, Lewin?" the guy asks, and shit, but that means Lewin's a dick for not remembering this guy's name. It's half-formed somewhere in his brain in that way, which means Lewin will recognize it the second he hears it again. But for the moment, he's drawing a complete blank, watching his smiling, beautiful face. He's probably the most beautiful person Lewin's ever seen in real life. *So it must be karma,* he thinks - someone this beautiful is too perfect for Lewin to have *good* sex with.

Lewin meets the guy's eyes and forces himself to smile back, watching a small, impossible frown line appear between the guy's eyebrows as he does so.

"I had a really good time," the guy says and then adds, "and I really hope you did too. Even though all evidence I have so far suggests otherwise." His smile says he's teasing - joking - but Lewin's not sure the steady look in his (striking, almost unsettling) eyes agrees. He wishes he knew this guy better so he could tell, and also wishes he could be gone already because this is a stress on his nerves he'd like to disappear from, please.

The guy continues, "I'd really like to see you again."

Lewin's face must give away how torn he feels - on the one hand: beautiful guy, way out of his league, who wants to see him again. On the other: horrible sex - because the guy pulls back further, leaving his hands gently holding onto

Lewin's arms. "You had a good time, right?" the guy says, and Lewin has enough practice with people in moments of stress (himself; Jacob; his mom) to recognize what heavily veiled panic does to a voice.

Lewin forces himself to say, "Yeah, no, of course." In what he's hoping will be a firm, confident voice, though sadly it isn't. The guy's face closes off a little, and, though he looks a little more steady than he did a second before, he still looks way more vulnerable than Lewin likes to be around by choice. Lewin pulls away and says, "You were great. It's just, it's me." And he's thinking, *how has this turned into a break up* as the guy folds his arms across his chest and raises a perfect, beautiful eyebrow in skepticism. "I just don't think I'm a casual sex guy."

The guy's face twists into an expression almost ugly - almost - for a split second, but then evens out as he offers a tentative smile, reaching out. "Well, there's an easy solution. Let's make it not casual."

Lewin laughs, once, bitterly, and instantly hates himself for the way it visibly makes this guy flinch, even as Lewin opens his mouth and says, "I don't even remember your name, pal." Hurt rises in the guy's eyes, and his frown deepens. Lewin fancifully thinks what this guy will look like in a few years: still beautiful, but with such an expressive face, he'll have laughter and frown lines and *fuck, why did the sex have to be bad?* Because Lewin could really like this guy, he thinks. He could have tried to, at least.

"Well, that's the worst nightmare," the guy says, smiling in a way inviting Lewin to laugh it off with him. "But you could ask."

Lewin has a bad habit of imagining his whole life with a person when he finds them attractive. Last night, he remembered being a few beers in and the guy flirting back with him and consciously not doing that, for once. Instead, he remembers just thinking, *this guy is too handsome to be real*, and making the most of it.

Now, he says nothing. Instead, just looks at the guy's hands still holding onto him.

The guy's jaw firms, and he pulls himself away and upright, closing off, even as he says, "Well, this has been a pleasure." He leans over Lewin's shoulder to the door to push it all the way open, then steps back and out of his reach. "See you around, Lewin."

Lewin pictures himself reaching out. Then, head bowed in contrition as he murmurs, "Sorry." And looks up at the guy through his eyelashes but doesn't think that's who he is or ever will be.

Instead, he turns on his heel and leaves, not looking back.

He walks across campus, avoiding the eyes of a girl holding her heels in one hand as he leaves the-guy-he'd-slept-wit's block. It's a warm, beautiful October morning, way earlier than Lewin usually sees, and every time (okay, the two times) he passes someone on their own, clearly in clothes from the night before, a small part of him wants to stop them and ask, "Was it less than you wanted, too?"

He makes it back to his block, seeing no one he knows. He just wants to fall into bed and fade into sleep for the next six hours, at least.

Unfortunately, his roommate is already up. He's wearing running gear and is stretching out - not sweaty yet, so he's on his way out. Lewin wishes he'd thought to stop off for coffee on his way back and missed this, but. Here they are.

He offers Jonas a faint smile, bracing himself for some good-natured ribbing, and sees Jonas' eyebrows go up as he looks Lewin over. All while doing a ridiculous stretch that makes Lewin's back ache just looking at it.

Lewin turns away, shrugging his jacket off, dropping his shoes on the floor where he takes them off because he knows it'll piss Jonas off and hopefully distract him long enough for Lewin to get into bed. Then he pulls his jeans off and does just that.

He can hear Jonas moving around behind him but stubbornly closes his eyes and ignores him. He feels itchy under the sheets, still wearing boxers and a t-shirt from the day before, and remembers he'd meant to go shower when he got back.

Well. He's in bed now, and Jonas hasn't left, still, so that's where he's staying.

"Lewin?" Jonas says, sounding unsure. "Lew?"

Lewin pulls the sheets up over his head, drawing his knees up closer to his chest. He's acting like a kid, but fuck it. He doesn't care anymore. He just wants to sleep and never think about last night again. He wants to not have to deal with Jonas' well-meaning obliviousness.

After a few quiet moments, Jonas moves. Lewin hears the door to their room open and shut, then hears him walking down the hall. Lewin lets himself have a moment to bring his hands up to his face and quietly scream into them in frustration, then turns, so he's facing the wall and tells himself, *sleep now; have a breakdown later.*

He's still awake, though, when the door opens again just a couple of minutes later. Lewin distinctly hears a ring pull and then feels someone Jonas-sized sit down on Lewin's bed in the space created by his curled-up legs.

Reluctantly, while cursing well-meaning idiot roommates, Lewin turns over onto his back to find Jonas, as he'd thought, holding an open can of Diet Coke so cold the condensation is misting around his fingers. He holds it out to Lewin, waiting patiently as Lewin rolls his eyes before pushing himself and his pillows up, so he's sitting cross-legged in his bed, facing Jonas.

He takes the Coke and sips from it.

"Thanks," he says begrudgingly. "I'm fine. Go on your run."

"Not until you tell me if I need to get hold of Campus Police," Jonas says, deadly serious. Lewin's never seen him anything close to serious, so it takes a second to register. So far, in the month and that they've known each other, Jonas has been affable, mostly, but oblivious; prone to getting so drunk he needs someone to look after him and to laughing at Lewin's jokes like he doesn't get them but wants Lewin to know he likes him. More recently, he's been trying to match Lewin's sarcasm with his own, but mostly he seems like he's not sure what to do with him. They don't have a lot in common. Still, he's far from the nightmare Lewin had feared he'd be when he first met him, wearing the fashionable sweatpants and snapback Lewin can never get right—looking every bit like someone who'd have shoved Lewin into any available hard surface last year. Even if the existence of another Lew in his life had meant Lewin had to go by his last name now, he's a good guy. Jonas had even taken the gay thing about as well as anyone Lewin's told.Lewin's being the slow one this morning, though, because he takes a few moments and a few sips of coke to figure out what Jonas means, and then he says, "What? No, Jesus, I'm fine."

"You sure?" Jonas asks. "Because it seems like you stayed out all night and came back looking like shit. No offense."

Lewin halfheartedly tries to kick him but finds he's too tangled in his sheets and gives up. "Offense taken," he mumbles. Then taps the can in his hand and asks, "Where'd you get this? Thought it was going to rot all the bones in my body."

Jonas shrugs. "Borrowed it from the kitchen," he says, which means he stole it. Lewin feels a little warm from that; he feels his lips involuntarily lift. "I'll pay it back!" Jonas insists, but he's smiling, too. "Come on," he adds. "What happened? Just tell me enough that I know if I should worry about you. Please."

Lewin shrugs, flipping the ring top back and forwards until it breaks off into the can. "I went home with a guy," he says.

"Okay," Jonas agrees, prompting him to go on rather than saying, *yeah, idiot, I'd guessed that part*, like Lewin would if their positions were reversed.

"We- fucked," he says, haltingly. "And it wasn't... I didn't... I don't know. It wasn't good?" He hears himself say it like a question and sees the concern on Jonas' face and cannot bear it, this whole situation. He wishes he'd just sucked it up and stayed with the guy, or come home last night, having never caught his eye. "It wasn't his fault. He was nice, and then I was a dick to him. Shit, I was a monster."

Jonas looks him right in the eyes and says, "That's not like you." With this faint curl to his lips that forces Lewin to smile along with him, then laugh.

"Fuck you," he says. "I am a *delight*."

Jonas is still laughing at his own joke but cracks up more at that, eventually getting himself under control to say, "Okay, but, 'wasn't good' like… awkward, neither of you knew what you were doing?"

Lewin hesitates, thinking, then says, "I guess. Yeah." The words are out before he realizes he's as good as admitted he's never done it before and flashes a panicked glare Jonas' way before reasoning it's not like his reactions up to that point had made it seem like he was an old hand at this stuff. Not the way he knows Jonas is. "It's not as easy to find someone to fool around with when you're gay in high school, okay? Straight people have it easy."

Jonas smiles benignly, holding his hands up in surrender, and waits until Lewin relaxes a little before he says, "maybe that's why it didn't go too well, then?" Jonas suggests. "The other guy probably had no idea what he was doing and the two of you just fumbled the catch a bit."

"Nice sports metaphor."

"Thanks," Jonas says. No way anyone's actually that oblivious to sarcasm. He does it on purpose half the time. Lewin is nearly sure.

"Maybe," Lewin says, uncertainty still clear in his voice.

"I don't know anyone whose first time went how they planned," Jonas continues, leaning back on his hands like he's getting comfortable and planning to stay a while. Lewin's surprised to realize he wouldn't mind if he did. "I made my prom date cry before mine," Jonas admits, half-smiling but nose scrunching a little in what looks like long-past guilt.

"Of course, you lost your virginity on prom night, you giant cliché."

"Hey," Jonas says, drawn out in indignation. "I nearly didn't, in the end, and it did not go how I planned, which is the moral of the story. I've had some *excellent* sex since then, and you will, too."

Lewin pulls his limbs up tight to his body as if he needs to be protected.

"How about I become a hermit instead?" he says, smiling as Jonas laughs like he's supposed to, and if Lewin is only half-joking, Jonas need not worry about that right now.

chapter

2

L ewin finished his last midterm half an hour ago, and he has just finally fallen into bed after what feels like a years' absence from it when there's one quick knock and his door is pushed open.

"I need you. Up," Jacob says, walking in and picking up the clothes Lewin has just taken off. Lewin is so blearily tired he's still struggling to process the magnitude of Jacob saying he needs him and what it does to his heart when Jacob adds, "Come on, I need a producer and you'll have to do."

Lewin stares at the hand Jacob is holding in front of his face and feels genuinely, deeply indignant. "Fuck you," he says. "I am running on negative sleep. Fuck off."

Jacob rolls his eyes, saying, "Nice statistic, Math Major. Come on, get up, we need to leave in five or we won't have time to grab a coffee on the way in, and then you'll really be pissed."

"Or I could sleep," Lewin says. "And you could go find literally *any*one else."

Jacob gives him an unimpressed look, dropping his shoes on top of him. "Like Jonas? He'll burn the studio down. Everyone else either has a midterm or is writing an assignment." Then, his expression softens, maybe taking in what state Lewin's in and says, "Look, I'm sorry. I would take it if there were any other options, but I need your help. Please."

Sometimes Lewin thinks Jacob figured out how weak Lewin is to him asking for things. If he has, though, Lewin comforts himself, Jacob's presumably spending a lot of his time feeling guilty for manipulating him.

As he should, because Lewin doesn't hold out against his puppy eyes for long. Finally, he says, "Ugh, fine, avert your eyes if you don't want an eyeful."

Jacob makes a show of leering at him until Lewin shoves him, pushing him out of the door with a parting, "Fuck you, pervert." Hopefully, hiding the flush, he can feel bloom up across the bridge of his nose.

Lewin pulls fresh clothes on, realizing the sweater is a Jonas hand-me-down when he has to push the sleeves up to the elbow. He catches a glance at himself in the mirror and snorts at the picture he makes; like he'd reached into a closet, blind, and worn whatever came out first.

When Lewin meets him at the door, Jacob beams opening his mouth to say something. Lewin cuts him off, saying, "Yeah, yeah, I have your eternal gratitude, I know; what will that buy me, though?"

Jacob snorts. "Not some new clothes, unfortunately."

"Oh, screw you," Lewin says and starts off on a rant about Jacob's sartorial choices and his fundamental hypocrisy in judging *anyone* else for what they wear. It carries them right up to when Jacob puts a coffee he's paid for in Lewin's hands. They start the short walk from the coffee place to the Union, falling into step because Jacob is one tall person who prides himself on being considerate.

Only then that Lewin notices Jacob's tense shoulders and his short answers and rebuttals to Lewin's points.

"What's got you twisted today?" Lewin asks. "Why does it even matter if you have a producer? You've managed on your own before."

Jacob pulls a face to show how much fun that hadn't been, and Lewin knows; he's done it a few too many times, too. Student radio is not a glamorous affair.

"I've got an interview," Jacob says.

"Okay?" Lewin says, finally, after waiting for there to be more to it. "I've produced for myself with three guests multiple times and never actually broken anything beyond repair, so you're going to have to find a better reason why you got me out of bed than that."

Jacob looks in the opposite direction as he shrugs. "I just want it to go well," he says. "This interview could be really good for us. Could lead to other things."

"Uh-huh," Lewin says. "So could me being in bed. Asleep."

"It was…" Jacob hesitating is a red flag. He looks almost sheepish, and Lewin can't think of the last time that's been true. "He's a cool guy, okay? It took a lot to get him to agree to come on, and he's really smart, and I don't want him coming on thinking it's amateur."

"That's kind of unavoidable," Lewin tells him, stalling because there's something more to this, but asking Jacob outright will get him nowhere. "Because it *is* amateur." He keeps watching Jacob, watching as Jacob gets more and more uncomfortable under his gaze, flushed but resolutely staring ahead as they round the corner into the Union.

Oh, Lewin thinks, suddenly realizing. *Jacob likes this guy.*

The knowledge sinks like a stone in Lewin's head. This nugget of something he's figured out about Jacob, added to the pile he hoards in his brain. This one lands heavily, and when he looks again at Jacob, he can't help but view him differently.

Had to happen eventually, he thinks. *Grow up; get over it.*

They come up the stairs towards the studio to see a figure waiting for them, sitting on the floor with a book propped up against his legs. Blond hair, glasses, lips perfect that describing them would sound too hyperbolic to belong to a real person.

"Hey, Quentin," Jacob says, sounding happy and relieved and a little breathless. Generally, the complete opposite of everything Lewin is feeling, meeting the eyes of a guy he rejected two years ago and who put him off sex maybe for forever. And who he hasn't seen since.

⸻ • ⸻

Cool day, Lewin thinks, faintly, as his tired brain catches up to the entire terror of the situation. He's in a booth with two very attractive men for the next two hours, stuck here, listening as they talk as if he isn't there. That alone is his worst nightmare. Ignoring the Quentin of it all, plus the Jacob, or the Jacob-and-Quentin, which apparently is a thing now? Something Lewin has to account for suddenly when he's never even imagined it could be possible up to now.

Fuck today.

"Lewin, are we ready?" Jacob asks.

"Sure," Lewin says, then actually checks whether they are or not. "Okay, I'll count you in," he says, making eye contact with Jacob and carefully ignoring Quentin. "Three, two, one..."

Jacob takes over smoothly, as if Lewin produces for him every week. Lewin is grateful that he doesn't because it means he's bad at it, and it takes all his concentration to do his job competently, and that means he has none left for the distractions in the room.

Especially the beautiful one boring holes into the side of his head.

It wasn't too weird that Lewin avoided talking to and looking at Quentin pathologically before Jacob's show. They'd had about five minutes to get set up and get the transfer from the show before theirs, and Lewin hasn't done this particular job very often. As a freshman, he'd been roped into doing all kinds of odd jobs - they all had - but now he, Jacob and Jonas run the whole operation, and they generally have freshmen to boss around for this kind of thing.

So Jacob only gives Lewin pointed looks when the show is done, and they've handed off to Olivia.

"What?" Lewin snaps at him. Already calculating how much time, he will get in bed tonight before the traditional end-of-midterms house party hits their apartment.

Jacob gives him a look that tells him he's being weird, a mix of exasperation and incredulity, before turning to Quentin and saying, "Thanks so much for coming on. You were great."

Quentin has a smug smile. It's probably not even something he can help, he just does, and he's still too attractive to even look at too long. Lewin wraps his own arms around himself and, after another pointed look from Jacob, finally says, "Hey, yeah, you were great. Jacob did good to get you to come on."

Quentin shifts from smiling at Jacob, saying, "Thanks, I had a great time." He's not being rude about it; it's not like his expression says Lewin is something disgusting he stepped on. He makes Lewin feel that way anyway, is all, and Jacob looking between the two with a faintly confused expression on his face is making this unbearable.

"I didn't expect to see you here," Quentin says, in a voice that says he's decided he's going for the kill. "You look good."

Lewin scowls. "Hey," he says defensively. "I had midterms right up to when Jacob forced me into helping out and I know I look like I can't dress,but that is not representative of me. Generally."

He stops short of saying *fuck you* only because Jacob is now looking between them with slowly dawning... horror? Delight? It doesn't seem like he's decided yet.

"You two know each other?" he asks.

"Barely," Lewin says, which is true but is also targeted to hurt, though Quentin's face is a blank, apathetic mask. *Biblically,* Lewin adds just for himself.

"We met in freshman year," Quentin adds. He's much calmer than Lewin feels, and he doesn't know exactly why, but all he's thinking is that he desperately doesn't want Jacob to discover his embarrassing encounter with this beautiful, smart, possibly perfect man.

So he, stupidly, runs. He says, "Oh, shit, I left…" And he breaks for the studio. He can imagine Jacob's bemused expression without seeing it, so he doesn't look as he pushes past them.

He remembers to open the door quietly. Olivia looks up as he enters, anyway. She smiles and says, "Hey." Which means she must have a record on.

Lewin smiles back. "Sorry, I just-" he says, and doesn't know how to end it.

She frowns at him and says, "Hey." This time with a trace of concern. "What do you need?"

"Nothing," Lewin says. Then corrects himself. "An excuse for why I needed to come back in here."

She raises her brows and stands to look out the window of the studio door, looking for what he was running from. "Oh," she says softly, and he doesn't know what she's put together, but he will not have time to tell her the whole story, even if he wanted to, before the record she's playing ends. So she gives him a sympathetic look all the same; it's a look that usually comes with people trying to hug him. She knows him better than to try, though, and instead, she says, "Well, I did need to run our next social past you. What do you think of a Rubik's cube party?"

"If it involves getting drunk and making Jonas try to solve one until he cries, count me in," he says, and she laughs, shushing him a second later so she can do a link between records.

"We should absolutely do that, too," she says finally, once that's done. "No, everyone comes with clothes of all different colors from a Rubik's cube and by the end of the night, you need to be wearing one solid color or you lose."

"Mandated clothes swapping," Lewin says. "Cool. Yeah, do it. First-person to manage it should get a prize."

"Of course. We should make a t-shirt or a pin or something," Olivia says, distracted a little by whatever she's setting up in here. Olivia's shows are a weird mix of politics, pop culture and crafts and right now she has a box that says it's a crochet kit in front of her alongside a close-up print-out of Bush's face, so who knows where that's going. He'll make Jacob put it on in the car on their way back to their place. She looks back up at him, searching his face for a moment. "There anything else I can do?"

Through the window, Lewin looks over his shoulder and sees Jacob standing against the wall on his own now.

He feels himself relax and turns back to her, smiling. "No, I'm good. Thanks."

"No problem," she says, smiling, mostly listening for the end of the record. "I'll see you tonight."

Nodding, Lewin leaves as quietly as he can again and meets Jacob saying with a bright, "Sorted!"

They talk their usual shit on the way home, and Lewin ignores the way Jacob's watching him more than normal. Lewin tells him, "Olivia manages to produce for herself, you know." Which is impressive as she narrates her attempts to crochet the President's likeness on the car radio.

"Thank you for helping," Jacob says, sounding catty and ungrateful. Then, in a tone that says he's trying to be casual but which misses the mark by a distance, he adds, "I didn't know you knew Quentin."

Lewin bites his cheek, noting they're nearly home and, just, couldn't Jacob have waited?

"Yeah," Lewin says. "You know, not really." He looks out the window and briefly wonders if asking Jacob to stop at Wendy's will end this conversation early or drag it out. Finally, he opts to stay quiet.

"I invited him to the party," Jacob says after a moment.

"Oh," Lewin hears himself say. "Okay." He tries telling himself it doesn't matter, that he'd only known the guy for less than half a day two years ago. That he's just built it up to be important in his head but that it isn't, and it shouldn't matter.

It's fine. It's just a guy who made Lewin question his whole identity. No big deal.

Jacob carefully turns onto their street, hands at two and ten, flicking a comparatively cautious glance Lewin's way before asking, "Is that okay?"

No, Lewin thinks, but says, "Sure." He means to add something to lighten the moment, but he just can't make himself say, *why wouldn't it be?* Because he's sure it'll come out strangled, weighed down with the dumb reasons it isn't.

"Okay," Jacob says, pulling into a spot next to their place.

Lewin is out of the car before Jacob puts it in park.

⋅⋅◆▬▬▬▬◆▬▬▬▬◆⋅⋅

Lewin wakes bleary-eyed and confused and with the sound of a party starting up no more than five feet away from his head, barely muffled by the thin walls of their apartment.

He gives himself the length of a song to stare at the ceiling and wish he didn't have to go out there, then pushes himself up, grabs an outfit he looks okay in, and heads to the bathroom for a quick, scalding shower and to give himself a pep talk in the mirror. It's not super effective, but after brushing his teeth, there's a loud knock on the door and a voice that says, "Hey, anyone in there?"

Lewin opens the door and lets Dresden in, taking his friendly clap on the shoulder with a smile. He forces himself into the party.

The apartment Lewin shares with Jonas and Jacob is where their group hangs out because it's criminally big for the money they spend on it, or at least the main room is. So the three make do with cupboard-sized bedrooms, each with a bed which takes up almost the entire floor space because their kitchen/diner/living room is twice the size of most of their friends' whole apartments. The downside is it always looks like a frat house exploded on it, but they have a tiny balcony for the smokers, too, so really, it's worth the compromises.

Now, most of their group have turned up, the music's on, and it's a welcoming little hub full of Lewin's friends he feels himself getting warm and fuzzy looking at despite himself. He finds Jonas pretty quickly and sticks to him like a barnacle. He gets a rant going about Jacob making him produce for him and makes Shannon laugh so hard she cries, which is cool. Shannon's new to their group, still, but if she's willing to laugh at his jokes, he's happy with Jonas settling down.

He's sure that's not what Jonas would call what's going on between the two, yet, but Lewin's got eyes.

Over Shannon's shoulder, Jacob moves into view. He's grinning, bright and wide, in a way Lewin sometimes gets to see when Jacob forgets about grades and his family and everything else he worries about and just focuses on whatever bullshit's coming out of Lewin's mouth to entertain him. He has to work hard for those grins, Lewin thinks and turns back to Jonas before having to see the source of the smile this time.

Lewin can't seem to avoid seeing Jacob, much as he tries. He sees him with a drink in his hand talking seriously to Anders, then dancing with Catrina, then with Quentin, who is laughing full-force and leaning into Jacob's space. Jacob is tall, is the thing. Even when he's sat down, he stands out, looking up at a dancing Rex and laughing at something he said. Lewin's eyes catch on how his shoulder is pressed into Quentin's.

Once he's noticed them together, they don't seem to separate, and Lewin can't stop staring at them like they're magnetic. Like he's orbiting them while they orbit each other.

Dumb, he tells himself.

He watches as Quentin leans in to say something directly in Jacob's ear, making Jacob's face smooth out from goofiness into something attentive. Jacob turns to Quentin and listens closely, then says something back, maybe asking a question, and looks like nothing could tear his attention away as Quentin replies.

"Are you okay?" Jonas asks in his ear, hand landing between Lewin's shoulder blades because when Jonas checks in, he can't help but do it partly through touch. He's a tactile guy. Honestly, Lewin made himself get used to it while they were still roommates as freshmen because he was so thrilled a straight guy would not be a dick about sharing his space. "You're kind of out of it."

Lewin thinks about lying. He thinks about saying, *sure, of course, don't smother me*, but Jonas and Shannon are both looking at him in confusion and concern and even as he's figuring out what to say he sees Jonas follow where he's been looking and the slow transformation of confusion to realization dawn on his face. He says, "wait, shit -"

"*Don't.*" Lewin glares at him, cheeks heating, as Shannon looks between the two with the calm, sympathetic look of someone who already knew this. Lewin guesses he hasn't been subtle. He's sure Jacob knows, and he knows Dresden does. Of their closest-knit group, Jonas is the last to get it.

Jonas holds his hands up and says, "Sure, okay, consider it unmentioned." Lewin knows that won't last, but Jonas manages a full minute before he asks, "Since *when?*"

"I'm not talking about this," Lewin tells him brightly, then pushes past Jonas towards the balcony.

He passes Jacob and Quentin to get there, keeping his head up and not looking away from his goal. He's pretty sure he hears Jacob say, "Hey, Lewin, did you know?" And he thinks Jacob reaches out and touches his thigh to get his attention, but Lewin plows on, and pretty soon, he's out on the balcony and away from all of it.

Olivia, Jenna and Boris are out there. The balcony's just big enough they can lay down on it next to each other and look up at the stars together, if they don't mind the cold of the tiles underneath them slowly seeping into their bones. They're giggling, drunk and sweet, Olivia's face pressed into Jenna's shoulder and Boris' arm is flung over her middle. The three are still giggling as they look up at Lewin, upside down, and as Olivia says, "Hey, Lewin."

Jenna and Boris greet him, saying, "Lewin's." He's never sure if those two are laughing more at or with him. Finally, he smiles, asking, "What're you doing out here?" As he sits on the ground next to their heads and leans back against the door, he'd slid closed behind him.

"Oh!" Olivia interrupts, reaching for and grabbing onto his ankle. "Are you okay? From earlier. What was going on?"

Lewin rolls his eyes and hits his head back against the glass of the door in exasperation, though a little harder than he'd meant to. "I'm fine," he says, but he's always found Olivia charming and drunk Olivia even more so, so he puts his hand on top of hers on his ankle to gentle the annoyance in his voice. "Thank you," he adds. "You saved me from awkwardness. That's all."

Olivia makes a noise that tells him she doesn't buy it, then asks, "Was it to do with Jacob flirting with that beautiful guy?"

Lewin glances at Boris and Jenna, who do not look surprised, then realizes he should've laughed it off if he were going to have any chance persuading any of them Olivia's off the mark.

"Oh, so everyone's talked about it," Lewin says. "Fantastic."

"Jonas hasn't caught on?" Olivia hazards, cut off by Lewin laughing without humor and asking, "What do you think I was running from just now?"

At least the stars are pretty.

Olivia reaches out for Lewin's hand with her free one, taking it and holding on. "I think the chances of him turning you down are pretty slim, love." And that's the worst part. Lewin's pretty sure she's right.

When Jacob came out to him last summer, they'd been day drinking to celebrate completing a sophomore year. Jacob had been working himself up to it all day when finally Jonas had gone inside to pee and Dresden had gone to grab them all drinks, and Jacob had turned to Lewin and said, "Hey, so I'm bi."

And Lewin had stared at him for a second before saying, "Shit, this is a real 'dear diary' moment, you know that?" And it'd taken him approximately one second to realize he's a dick for somehow making Jacob's big moment about himself and the same amount of time for Jacob to laugh, hard, letting out all the tension he'd been holding until he's nearly crying it out. He'd pulled Lewin into a one-armed hug and said, sincerely, "Thank you." And Lewin hadn't been able to look at him as he'd laughed awkwardly and replied, "No, thank you for telling me. It's a big thing."

Jacob had pulled away, looked at Lewin side on, and asked, "Does it get less big? I feel like when you told us it was no big deal."

Lewin had shrugged, then considered it, and while considering Jacob's question, he'd got caught up in wondering if he was the first person Jacob had said it out loud to and can't stop the honored, touched feeling he gets in his heart.

"You know how ducks look like they aren't making an effort when they swim, but if you look under the surface, their legs are going crazy?" Lewin had asked, tipsy enough his analogies are coming out of him without permission. "Their chicks don't swim like that, do they? I think it's like that. You get better at pretending it's no big deal, but the anxiety never goes away." He'd looked at Jacob to find him looking faintly overwhelmed, and Lewin had said, "Sorry, that's probably not what you need to hear. I am not the best ambassador for the community."

"No, it's honest," Jacob had said after a moment's thought. He'd grinned, shy but bright, and added, "Lewin, I think this is an actual, human-to-human moment you're letting us have, here. I didn't know you had it in you."

"Fuck off, I'm plenty human," Lewin had said, shoving at Jacob's shoulder. Objectively, it's one of the stupider things he's ever said, but it'd made Jacob laugh and Dresden, as he'd rejoined them, say, "Huh, who would've guessed."

Jacob had told Dresden and Jonas that same afternoon, growing more confident with it each time. Jonas had taken a moment to process it but had come through like the earnest puppy he is at heart, and Lewin remembers seeing the relief in Jacob and being bowled over by how much he'd cared about the idiot.

That's maybe where it'd started.

Lewin had been flirting innocently with both Jacob and Jonas since he'd decided they were his best friends, and there was nothing he could do about it, so after Jacob's revelation, Lewin had been careful not to stop. And from there, he'd dug himself a hole.

"Maybe," he says now to Olivia. "But maybe not, so I can't. I'll get over it," he adds, flashing her a smile, then turning to Boris for a reliable distraction. "Hey, who won Best Supporting Actress at the Oscars in 1969?"

"Ruth Gordan, *Rosemary's Baby*," Boris replies immediately. "And I see what you are doing, Lewin, so you'd better at least think of some difficult ones if you want me to go along with this distraction."

Lewin laughs, joining Olivia and Jenna, and gives Jenna a grateful look when she says, "Best Screenplay, '67."

Lewin figures this can only get better if he's high, so he shares a little of Olivia's weed-stuffed pipe until he's giggly-sad instead of just sad.

As a veneer of normalcy, it probably needs work.

"Do I have to?" he asks, whining, as Jenna stands in front of him and waits for him to move.

"Lew," she says. "I need food, and food is inside. You have to."

"Ugh."

He rolls out of the way and onto his feet, helped by the balcony railing. He holds onto it tightly and leans over a little to look down at the ground until Boris puts a hand on his shoulder, turning him round to face the three, serious-faced.

"We'll flank you," Boris tells him. "Don't worry, love. It'll be fine."

"I'm fine," he says, but it's not like he's trying to persuade them. He rolls his eyes at himself and pastes on a grin. "Don't I seem fine?"

Jenna says, "Oh, babe." Walking the thin line between sympathetic and done with his shit. She wraps an arm around his waist, letting him wriggle free but still stay close as the four head back into the party. Jenna beelines straight to the kitchen, where there's a cooling selection of pizzas on the counter, and they follow.

Lewin sees Jacob leaning against the refrigerator too late. Jacob looks up, grinning slow and easy at him, and Lewin can't turn away now. He detours enough to grab two slices of pizza - different toppings - and stacks them into a sandwich before Jacob says, "Hey, where've you been tonight?" And looms into Lewin's space.

"Balcony," Jenna says shortly, around a mouthful of pizza. She settles next to Lewin, eyes trained on Jacob in that unsettlingly aware, fixated way high Jenna gets sometimes.

Jacob looks between them. "Cool," he says. "It's nice out there." He seems to have forgotten exactly how to talk like an intelligent person, which often happens to him around Jenna. Boris loops an arm around Jacob's neck and hangs off him, smiling too-sweetly at him, and Jacob maybe actually blushes. It's hard to tell in this light - they've just got the lamps in the corners of the room on because the lounge light is out again - but Lewin's pretty sure. Having Boris and Jenna's attention on a single person is cruel, really.

"So, who's your pretty boy?" Boris asks in a stage whisper. Now Jacob is definitely blushing up to his neck, which is both Lewin's favorite and least favorite version of Jacob, because he's basically impossible to look away from.

"He's uh, an attractive guy, sure," Jacob says as if he's only just thinking about it. "Good face."

"You're still so bad at gay talk," Lewin says. It's meant to be a joke, but that's not how it comes out. Boris flicks him a quick, surprised glance, and Jacob frowns a little, looking more confused than anything. Lewin shoves half of his pizza sandwich into his mouth in an effort to be less of a monster.

"Okay," Jacob says, slow. His face is torn, like he's still figuring out if he should be offended by that or laugh it off. Lewin briefly wishes Jonas were here to model for Jacob that they should be making fun of Lewin. That it should be a *Lewin, you don't have a monopoly on being gay* situation, not a situation where they fight or Jacob looks upset.

Then again, it's probably better for them all that Jonas, with his expressive, never-learnt-to-lie face is nowhere near the two for the rest of the night.

Pizza has never tasted so awful.

"So?" Boris prompts, turning so he's half-shielding Lewin with his own body as if Jacob's a bomb that's about to go off. He's looking at Jacob with feigned impatience. "You haven't driven him away, have you? Because I have to warn you: if you have, he's fair game for the rest of us."

Lewin morosely takes another bite of pizza, surreptitiously glancing up at Jacob to see him looking uncomfortable but amused. Like with Jenna, that's pretty much how Jacob gets around Boris.

"Not yet," Jacob is saying. "I'll point him in your direction if and when, though."

"Oh, as if. Don't humor me," Boris says, sounding pleased. "*You're* punching above your weight with that one."

Lewin sees Jacob shake his head, smiling, from the corner of his eye and tries to focus on Jenna's arm brushing against his to stop from dropping his pizza on the floor, grabbing Jacob by the neck of his stupid, too-tight polo and kissing him on the lips.

His imagination stalls from there. He's kissed people before; he doesn't know why when he imagines it happening again, a white noise machine turns on in his brain.

That time with Quentin - that *only* time - wasn't traumatic enough for him to be this messed up over it.

It wouldn't have been for anyone else, anyway.

"Hey."

Quentin - pink-cheeked, grinning, and with shining eyes - slots into their formation beside Jacob in a space that could've been intentionally left for him. He gives a wave that should be awkward to the group, then a nod to Lewin as his smile dims. "Hi everyone. Lewin."

Jacob introduces them all, telling everyone about the interview that afternoon and how cool Quentin's extracurricular work writing about the Sudan or something is. He breaks off, though, to say, "Hey, you never explained how you two know each other…" leading, looking between Quentin - who Lewin now sees, looking up, has been watching him since he slotted next to Jacob - and Lewin.

Quentin's smile is as noncommittal as they come, but something about the way he holds eye contact with Lewin in the pause after Jacob's question makes Lewin's heart kick up a gear. His hands get clammy, and he decides he has to talk to Jacob.

He tosses the crusts of his pizza on the counter behind him and grabs Jacob by the arm. "I need to talk to you," he says, pulling him out of the kitchen and towards their rooms.

He imagines if he looked around, he'd see Quentin watching them with that same noncommittal smile, but he doesn't know the guy, really. Maybe that's dumb.

"Hey, Lewin, what the hell?" Jacob asks, letting himself be pulled along, which Lewin's not kidding himself. No way he'd be able to move Jacob if he didn't want to be moved.

Lewin hesitates in front of their bedroom doors before finally choosing the neutral ground of Jonas' room, sending up a prayer of thanks when it's not the site of something he never wants to see between Jonas and Shannon, yet.

He drops Jacob's arm. Folds his own across his chest.

"Have you done it with a guy, yet?" he asks Jacob, all in a rush.

There's a beat of silence in which Lewin prepares for Jacob to either laugh or shout at him, but what he gets instead is just as Jacob in its own way.

"I take it you mean 'have I had sex with a man yet'?" Jacob translates. He sighs, sitting heavily on Jonas' bed, bouncing a little with the force of it. He sighs again, less genuine this time, put on to lighten the mood or just make this less intense. "Yeah. Why?"

Lewin bites his lip as if he needs extra help from his own body not to answer that. He shrugs. Some of the tension leaves him, though.

"You want details?" Jacob asks a wry, sarcastic twist to his mouth that says he knows the answer. Lewin snorts and shakes his head anyway. Jacob tilts his head like a Labrador. "Is this where you give me the gay birds and the bees?" he asks.

"Pretty sure that analogy only works where reproduction is involved," Lewin says. "But yeah, I guess. If you'd needed it, I'd have made sure you knew what to expect."

Lewin would like to run out of the window to his left to escape this conversation, now, before Jacob asks questions, but Jacob smiles and looks kind of fond - touched by the gesture - even as he's clearly exasperated.

"You know there's this thing called the internet…" Jacob says. Lewin automatically responds, "Oh, yeah, and you should definitely trust everything that's said on there." To which Jacob just laughs, fondness winning out on his face.

"Thanks for the thought," he says. He stands up. "Was that it?"

Lewin should say yes, and shrug, and maybe break out some blackmail material so Jacob never mentions this conversation to anyone. But he wants to say, *if you don't like it-*

He cuts off the thought. Because he's sure, deep down, it wasn't Quentin. He's pretty sure it had nothing to do with Quentin. He's sure Quentin did nothing wrong. He's sure Jacob will be absolutely fine, because he's known all along, deep down, that it's just him that's messed up.

Lewin's been quiet too long, and Jacob looks confused and concerned, now, all the fondness hidden away.

"Hey," Jacob says, reaching out as if he will touch Lewin's waist. "You said you were okay with him being here," he adds. There's a loaded pause in which Lewin knows Jacob's thinking things through from every angle. "Is it not okay?" Then, softer says, "If it's not, tell me."

It's weird that two guys I've made into these big things in my head are all over each other, Lewin thinks, and then traps the thought away where it can't make Jacob sad.

He shakes his head gives Jacob a tight-lipped smile that's just as effervescent as he can make it with the balloon of trapped emotion sitting between his ribs and his stomach. "No, it's fine. Sorry," he says. "I'm just spacey; you know what Olivia's stuff is like."

Jacob laughs on queue; says, "Right. Now it makes sense."

He guides Lewin back out into the party, where Lewin continues to blame the pot and convinces himself it's why he can't feel his feet or face or anything but burning, inappropriate jealousy, and hurt as he watches Quentin and Jacob go back to orbiting each other.

Jacob slots back into the space Quentin has left at his side, shares a loaded glance with him, and drops a too-casual arm over his shoulder.

They both look overly pleased with themselves.

Lewin picks up a bottle of the worst liquor to hand - tastes like aniseed - and drinks straight from the bottle until Olivia - kind-eyed, dancing Olivia - takes it away and leads him out of the gravitational pull of the two brightest boys in the room.

◦•◗▬▬▬▬▬◆▬▬▬▬◖•◦

Later, as these things tend to go, he regrets everything.

He's in a bathroom again - this time his own - and the early morning light is filtering in through the blinds, and he's deciding whether he will throw up again if he moves when the door behind him opens and Quentin says, "Oh, shit, sorry." Then, after a pause, "Are you dying?"

"I wish," Lewin says, before he realizes who he's talking to. Then he groans, dropping his head down to the porcelain with a thunk that says it's plastic. He says, "Just put me out of my misery."

"One of those morning afters, huh?" Quentin asks, amusement clear in his voice. Lewin's *I'm being laughed at* senses are tingling, and that's something he'll maybe have the energy to care about after twelve more hours of sleep.

"Yes." He pushes himself up until he's sitting upright. Quentin watches him, concerned and amused in what is a common look shared by anyone watching a harmless drunk person, until Lewin says, "I'll move, sorry. Just give me a sec." Before closing his eyes and trying to get up to his feet without opening them in the hopes it'll make him feel less like he's at sea.

"Wait," Quentin says, grabbing onto Lewin's elbow to steady him.

His hands are smaller than Jacob's. Nearly as small as Lewin's. One of the last things Lewin remembers, semi-coherently, is one of those hands curled in the short hairs at the nape of Jacob's neck as they'd walked out of the lounge towards Jacob's room.

As soon as he's standing roughly under his own power - the wall is helping a little - he shrugs Quentin off.

Keep your filthy paws off my silky drawers, Lewin thinks, nonsensically, so either Rex or Olivia must've put *Grease* on last night at some point. That or Lewin is spontaneously quoting Rizo, now, internally, which really would be cause for an end to it all.

"Did we watch *Grease?*" he asks.

The short laugh sounds like it's forced out of Quentin in sheer surprise before he says, "Yeah, pretty sure you guys woke up the whole block singing about your automatic, systematic, hydromatic cars."

Oh. So after they went to bed, then. Lewin thinks. *Probably.* His head hurts too much to think on it too much more, which is a blessing in a very good disguise.

"Come on," Quentin says. "Let's get you some water."

He pulls Lewin through to the lounge somehow without actually touching him - pure magnetism, maybe - and sits him on the couch before raking through the kitchen until he brings back a big, novelty cereal bowl for any hypothetical vomit, a pint glass of water, and some saltines. He arranges everything around Lewin before looking at him contemplatively for a moment and sitting down next to him. He twists slightly so he's facing him.

"You should drink that," he says, watching Lewin through a blank mask of a face, giving away none of the annoyance or disgust Lewin's sure he must be feeling. Lewin obediently picks up the glass of water, brings it to his lips, and closes his eyes in ecstasy as he sips the cool water.

"Thanks," Lewin says. He keeps his eyes closed as he lowers the glass to hold it between his knees and curves his back over it, resting his face in his hands, pressing into his eye sockets in the effort to make them hurt less. "You don't have to stay with me. I'm not actually dying."

"It's fine," Quentin replies.

They stew in awkward quiet for a few long minutes, Lewin extra conscious of Quentin being right next to him, so close it'll take actual effort not to touch him when he eventually feels up to standing up again. That's not likely to happen soon, though; he'll be crawling back to his room if he has to move any time in the near future.

"So, is it a full blackout or just a partial situation?" Quentin asks eventually, reaching for the saltines and offering them to Lewin before taking a couple himself.

"Pretty total, I think," Lewin tells him. He chances a glance at Quentin to find him slouched back on the couch, watching Lewin with half-lidded eyes. There's a shadow where his shirt opens at his neck that could be a hickey. He looks away. "Were Jonas and Dresden trying to get us all to play drunk Trivial Pursuit at one point?"

"Not when I was around," Quentin says, and it might just be a trick of Lewin's pickled brain, but his voice is a little harder when he says it, he thinks. Or maybe just a little more intense.

Lewin says, "Right, that was after you." He waves toward the bedrooms. "Of course."

His brain isn't tricking him over how he says that; his voice comes out timid and hurt, and his shoulders tense up, and Quentin's not an idiot because Jacob would never be attracted to him if he were, so obviously he's going to notice.

"Jacob said you were okay with it," Quentin says, with that same intensity and a little surprise.

"You guys talked about me?" Lewin turns his head to look at him and instantly regrets it as his head pounds. He reaches for the cereal bowl, just in case. Quentin is still lounging, somehow only his voice giving away that he's interested in their conversation. Unless Lewin's ears are playing tricks on him.

"Of course," Quentin says. "You're best friends, and whatever grudge you might hold against me, I didn't want to mess anything up between you two, so I asked him if he was sure you were okay with it, and he said you'd said you were."

"Grudge?" Lewin asks. Quentin looks at him in askance, as if the answer to that one-word question were obvious. Lewin doesn't want to admit how confused he is, so instead just focuses on the important part. "Yeah, I'm fine with… you and him," he says. "Good for you. Please spare me the details."

There's a pause while Lewin looks into the depths of his cereal bowl and contemplates the likelihood of him vomiting into it before this conversation blessedly ends. Then Quentin says, "You must have been more convincing when you weren't hungover because Jacob seemed really sure."

Sure is both the opposite of how Lewin feels right now and how Quentin sounds. Lewin glances at him out of the corner of his eye to see that Quentin has now tipped his head back and is staring at the ceiling, frowning hard, teeth pulling at the pink fullness of his bottom lip.

"It's fine," Lewin says, trying one more time to sell it.

"It's obviously not," Quentin tells him. "Please stop lying."

Lewin makes a frustrated sound that's half-sigh, half-laugh, and says, "You hardly know me. Can't you just take it at face value when I tell you what's going on inside my head?"

"No," Quentin says. "You're right, but I still know you're not okay with me and Jacob and I don't know why you didn't tell him that. Did you even tell him how we knew each other? I stupidly assumed you must have when you dragged him off for that one-to-one, but obviously I should have checked with him."

Quentin's speaking quicker and quicker. Finally, when he breaks off, he's sitting up again, turned towards Lewin on the couch, and leaning towards him, trying to make eye contact.

"Open communication is important before sex," Lewin agrees, to be a dick.

"Fuck you," Quentin says in a quick, brief flash of anger.

Lewin flinches, mentally kicks himself, then turns and says, "I'm sorry." That feels like not enough, but he stumbles over what else to say. He wants to throw up; thinks of the relief from nausea he might feel in the aftermath if this sick to his stomach feeling were only caused by drink. Finally, he adds, "I said that to be hurtful, and you didn't deserve it."

Lewin remembers seeing that exact facial expression - a small crease between his eyebrows, biting his lip, eyes wide - on Quentin's face two years ago as he left him on his doorstep. It hasn't got any more bearable with time.

Lewin goes to take a drink only to find he's run out of water. His throat is scratchy and dry, and he mournfully thinks about getting up to get more - at least he'd be able to give Quentin some space - but Quentin loudly exhales, exasperatedly, and takes the glass from him. He's gone for a moment, returning with a full glass of cool water.

"Here," he says, holding it out. It could be a peace offering or it could just be water, but Lewin is tentatively hopeful as he takes it, holds Quentin's eyes, and says, "Thank you."

Quentin sits back down next to Lewin.

"I'm sorry you aren't okay with it," Quentin tells him. "You should know, I was hoping to make out with someone in front of you to show you I was over it, and I like Jacob, but I wouldn't have slept with him if I'd known it would hurt you."

Lewin tries to make a sound of agreement, but he's sure it sounds a lot less okay and nonchalant than he'd like.

"Was it that it was Jacob?" Quentin asks. "Or that it was with me?"

"You say that like it can't be none of the above," Lewin replies. Quentin just looks at him, steady and sure of his conclusions, waiting for Lewin to blink. Lewin looks away, shrugs once, and then says, "It's really not your problem. Just go back to bed. Enjoy it."

Quentin takes that in, still, laser-focused on Lewin - so intent and single-minded Lewin can feel his eyes on the side of his head like they're pinning him to a specimen board.

"Okay, well," he says, after a long pause where Lewin refuses to look at him. "That sucks, but okay. You don't have to worry. I'll, uh, get out of your way. Least I can do for an old acquaintance."

"What?" Lewin stares at Quentin in absolute incredulity. Either he's not capable of following a conversation with this many layers or Quentin is… an idiot? Or very sweet. Lewin's not sure which idea would be more devastating. "What are you talking about?"

Quentin's smile *is* sweet, knowing and a little bit mocking, but it's as likely to be mocking of himself as of Lewin.

"Are you telling me you got blackout drunk *not* because you have a thing for Jacob?" Quentin asks. The way he asks should be condescending. It is, really. Lewin will work up to being incensed about it, maybe, once he's done reeling from his gut reaction which is to say, "What? No." again. Quentin lazily shrugs before saying, "Okay, I don't know you. Maybe you get blackout drunk all the time. It just doesn't seem true to type."

"What's that supposed to mean?" Lewin asks, realizing he's pulled his legs up so one's under him and he can cling to the other with both arms. Fuck. His head's too vulnerable for this conversation.

"I… don't know," Quentin admits, sounding a lot less condescending now. He's watching Lewin, and seems taken aback by his body language. He offers Lewin a smile like a peace offering. "I really don't know you that well. I'm kind of a snap judgment sort of person, and my snap judgment of you wasn't that you were surviving college via an alcohol dependency." He pauses, grimaces, and starts again in an almost different tone. "Sorry. All of that makes me sound like a judgmental dick. I normally don't think like this, and I definitely don't talk like it. I'm in a weird mood."

Quentin's been so self-assured throughout the short time Lewin's spent with him that it's a shock to hear him unsure and self-deprecating. *Shit,* Lewin thinks. *I've been adjacent to two fine one-night stands in Quentin's life and I've ruined both. Hopes he's at least had some ordinary, well-adjusted experiences between.*

"I drink a normal amount, so your snap judgments aren't wrong," Lewin admits after a longer pause. "Sorry. About being a mess. It's really not your problem."

Quentin shrugs and smiles with half of his mouth, wryly, as if it's no big deal, eyes keen as he continues to watch him.

"Have you been… pining?" Quentin asks, straight-faced like that's something you can just ask someone. Lewin pulls a face to show what he thinks of that idea.

Then he shrugs, and says, "I've been… noticing, I guess. He's my best friend and he's *that* hot and he's not even straight. I noticed." He shrugs again. "And, again, not your problem. Go enjoy some, you know, morning after sex, or whatever."

Lewin pretzels himself up, so he's not hugging himself anymore but is still as tightly wound in a chair as it's possible to be.

"I think he's noticed back," Quentin says softly. He watches Lewin as he fidgets and won't meet his eyes, then exhales loudly in put-on frustration and says, with a wry smile, "God, this sucks. Why are the good ones always taken?"

Lewin snorts a laugh into his water. "He's not! I haven't- I've said, haven't I? Have at it. Get yourselves to a courthouse and get some civil partnership paperwork rushed through for all I- well, for all I get a say in any of this, which is not at all, because my stuff is *not your problem.*"

When Quentin just continues to watch him, Lewin asks, "Are you always this self-sacrificing? It's dumb. Nothing good is going to come from it. I'm going to start thinking you don't even like him in a minute, and then I'll be really pissed because you should know now Jacob isn't a casual kind of person. That civil partnership bit was only mostly a joke."

"Sounds like you two are a match made in heaven," Quentin says, his smile growing a little more sly. "Given you once told me you're not a casual kind of person, either."

Lewin is a bear when a trap snaps around its legs and hobbles it, left blinking owlishly at Quentin. He pulls himself out of the metaphor and looks away, down at his hands where they're twisting the material of his shirt until it's pulled unflatteringly taught against his waist.

Trapped, he does what he always does when he feels out of control.

"I lied. I just didn't want to see you again," Lewin tells him. "Sorry. I was and am a dick when it comes to that kind of thing." He pauses, leaving the moment of honest-meanness to hang in the space between them. "Did you get that in your snap judgment assessment?"

"That, what, you actually don't do commitment?" Quentin asks. "I figured there was a reason you weren't letting yourself have what you obviously want." He's strangely level, still. Lewin wishes he didn't want to get under his skin, but that's what he wants, now, glancing up at Quentin's calm, steady expression. "I think it's dumb not to try."

Lewin meets his eyes. "So take your own advice. Go get back into bed."

Reaching for the TV remote, Quentin turns it on and flips through the channels until he settles on one where the Roadrunner is falling to their death. He puts the remote back, turns to Lewin, and says, seriously, "This is my favorite, and if you change the channel, I will take it very personally." He gets up, takes Lewin's empty water glass, and leaves for a few minutes. Lewin watches the TV in an absent, confused state, unsure where he'd expected that conversation to go or where it actually ended up.

When Quentin returns, it's with a newly filled water glass - which he hands to Lewin - and quietly says, "Jacob's coming through in a few minutes, so you'd better decide now."

Lewin takes the water on autopilot. He stares as Quentin sits down next to him, leaving a Jacob-sized space between them, then Lewin says, "I think I may throw up."

Quentin passes him the empty cereal bowl.

Lewin is curled up on the couch, tucked as far into the cushions as he can get, when Jacob emerges, giving both identical sleepy, happy smiles. He has his comforter wrapped around his shoulders and sits between the two, taking up the whole space so Lewin wishes he could sink into a space between the cushions and the arm of the couch.

"Morning." Jacob looks between them, eyes crinkled into a smile but obviously confused, too; it's visible in the way he's biting his lip. "Good night?" he asks Lewin, taking in the state he's in, obviously amused.

Lewin shrugs. "Oh, sure," he says. "Though you'll have to ask one of the people who let me get too drunk to remember my own name to find out why it was so great." He cuts a glance at Quentin, who carefully watches the two. He gives Lewin a brief, unreadable look. One that seems to dare him.

And there's a huge, screaming part of Lewin that wants to turn to Jacob right now and say, "Hey, leave this Ken Doll perfect man and have me, your annoying, hard-work best friend instead." Or maybe he just wants to kiss him, vomit breath be damned.

"Anyway," he says. "You had a better one, I hear." And waggles his eyebrows.

Jacob laughs, delighted and even looking a little relieved (*cool, I didn't need that ego anyway*, Lewin thinks, thinking fatalistically that all the times he thought maybe Jacob felt the same must actually just have been a cruel trick of suggestion and false hope like he'd always feared). Jacob blushes right across his nose. He turns to look at Quentin, a grin breaking across his face, starting shy and quickly building to just… happy.

"I've definitely had worse," Jacob says, flirting while sounding somehow sweet and wholesome.

He leans into Quentin's space, watching to see if it's okay as he does so, and gives him a sweet, lingering kiss, looping an arm around his shoulders.

Quentin sighs against his lips, suddenly relaxed in himself in a way he hadn't been the whole time he'd been alone with Lewin, Lewin now realizes.

And Lewin watches them, cartoons on in the background until they break away from each other and give him near-identical sheepish looks.

"Want some pointers?" Lewin asks, just to get them to stop looking at him like that, especially Quentin, and manages a smile when Jacob laughs and swats at him with a couch cushion.

The three settle in, Jacob sharing his comforter with Quentin and the two curling into each other; Lewin on the other side of the couch, curling into himself. The cartoons roll on, and Lewin promises himself he won't let the roiling pit of jealousy ruin either a chance for these two beautiful, intelligent people to be happy or one of the most important relationships in his life.

There's something fucked up about watching cartoon characters fight in an endless loop and thinking, *what a lovely metaphor for how watching this happen is going to feel.* Lewin is a fan of self-serving metaphors, but he'd be happy if this one turned out to be just the product of a melodramatic, hungover brain.

He just doesn't think watching Jacob with someone else will ever stop feeling like an anvil dropping on his head.

chapter

Quentin has known this from the start: the only time it'll be okay for him to tell Jacob is *now*. Right at the beginning.

He's pretty pissed Lewin left it for him to do, actually. Or he would be, if he didn't understand how excruciatingly awkward it must be for Lewin, right now. Being okay with Quentin-and-Jacob. Being (normal) around them. Pretending he's not pining after his best friend. He does understand why Lewin doesn't want to add explaining to that best friend that his current boyfriend is someone who he fucked, once.

He gets it, but he's still kind of pissed.

Quentin and Jacob have been dating, or whatever it is they're doing, for a week when Quentin hits an internal deadline he set for himself and that his mom will ask him about the next time she calls. A point of no return, he calls it in his head. So on a Friday after his last class, he knocks on Jacob's (and Lewin and Jonas) door and says, "Did I ever tell you how Lewin and I knew each other?" As soon as he sees Jacob's goofy smile on his perfect face.

"Uh… no?" Jacob says, letting Quentin step under his hand on the door after an exchange of quick pecks on the lips - they start with one, but both go back for an extra. "Which you know, because your memory is stupid good."

Quentin peeks into the main room, waving to Jonas and Shannon, before snagging Jacob's hand in his and leading him to his own room. He sits on Jacob's bed, laughing as Jacob stands between Quentin's knees and kiss him properly for a good few minutes, his back bent over to make up for the height difference.

Jacob is… really sweet. And funny. And smart. And *hot*. And Quentin needs to rip this band-aid off and discover if there's a festering wound underneath now, not later, because later might lead to a broken heart. Or at least to some inadvisable life choices. He doesn't have a good track record on that score with boys in this apartment, but he's hoping he's actually learned something since he was a dumb eighteen-year-old, excited to be having a normal college experience and excited to be queer.

Jacob lets him pull away with a pout. He leaves one hand touching Quentin's jaw (and occasionally his lips); the other plays with his fingers.

"I met Lewin in freshman year," Quentin says, watching Jacob's face without ever meeting his eyes. "Well, his freshman year. My honorary one. We hung out one day, got day-drunk and then slowly sobered up together, and I convinced myself he was the smartest, funniest, strangest guy I'd ever meet." Jacob's eyes, Quentin can tell by what the rest of his face is doing, have widened in realization. Quentin twists his mouth into a self-deprecating smile. "I convinced myself I was half in love with him, and we spent the night together. Then in the morning, he rejected me and didn't even remember my name and I spent most of the year pining over him because I was pathetic, and then finally, I got over it. And him."

Quentin stops. Then waits. Jacob's still holding onto his hand and his face, but he's stopped moving, and Jacob seems to be sort of staring off into space.

"Oh," Jacob says. "Huh."

He doesn't sound pissed off, probably, but there's only so much a person can glean from two syllables.

"I'm sorry," Quentin says. "One of us really should have told you that first night. I assumed he had, actually. But I should've told you then, and I've probably left it too late to only tell you now. I don't know. I'm sorry."

Jacob sits down next to Quentin, hand falling from his face to instead help the other one out in wrapping itself around

Quentin's one hand. The body language which Quentin takes as a good sign, all things considered, though he's not ready to put on an annual parade to his and Jacob's beautiful future just yet.

"Well, you didn't have to," Jacob says. "We haven't… talked yet. About what we're doing. So there'd be no obligation for you to have told me." He turns to Quentin, flashes him a quick smile - genuine, but unsteady. "Thank you, though."

Quentin nods, feeling unsteady himself. "I wanted to have that conversation but couldn't until you knew. Is it weird for you?"

"Kind of," Jacob admits, stroking his thumb across Quentin's knuckles and back again. "Lewin's really private about this kind of stuff, so… it's the first time something like this has come up. So it's a little weird." He pauses, looking at nothing in particular as a crease appears between his eyebrows. "Makes sense why you two were so awkward when you 'met', though. Do you still like him?"

Quentin bites his own cheek to keep a straight face.

"I didn't even know him for a full twenty-four hours," he says. "So no. Not like I like you." He can't stop himself from flashing a quick, shy smile at Jacob, and glows somewhere deep in his chest when it's returned. "But. I hadn't had sex before him, so I'll always remember that fondly. If that's a problem, you should say now."

Jacob frowns. "Uh, no," he says. "You get to remember whatever you want with as much fondness - or love, even - as you feel. Even if we decide we're dating, I don't have a monopoly on your past."

Quentin's mouth splits into a grin. He fights the urge to duck his head, loving instead how pink blooms across Jacob's cheeks as he sees how good of an answer he just gave; how happy Quentin is with him.

"In that case," Quentin says. "If you're sure you're okay with the Lewin thing, I'd like us to be dating. Boyfriends. If you're up for that."

"Yeah," Jacob says, leaning in for a kiss. "Yeah, I'm up for that," he says again, pausing their kiss just long enough. He pulls back again a minute later. "Exclusive?" he asks, nudging Quentin's nose with his own.

"Sure, okay," Quentin says, through a grin and a kiss.

"Cool, good," Jacob says, just as muffled. They say little for a while, then.

"You and Lewin, huh?" Jacob asks a little while later, his face performing an intense vacillation between emotions.

"You look like you still can't decide if you find it hot or if you should be jealous."

"Um. Maybe?" Jacob says it like a question but has squeezed his eyes shut and is laughing at himself already. "Shut up. Is that weird?"

Quentin shrugs, kissing Jacob's neck. "I don't care," he says. "I'm into you and whatever you're into."

And maybe when he tells his mom about this, she'll be a little concerned and laugh at him a lot, but Quentin's pretty sure she'll also tell him to do whatever makes him happy.

And if what makes him happy right now is to make Jacob laugh and blush so badly he hides his face in his own hands by whispering certain things in his ear about Jacob's best friend, then so be it.

chapter

74

"You know, I think the point of hate sex is to hate the other person, not what you're doing."

Lewin rolls his eyes hard, stomach dropping harder. He pulls away from Troy, getting his hand off Troy's dick with some relief and a lot of burning self-hatred.

"I think the point of someone touching your dick is just to shut up and enjoy it," Lewin tells him.

Troy leans up over Lewin on his elbow, pants around his knees, and cock hard against his stomach. His shirt's pushed up over an enviably flat belly dotted with freckles, and Lewin is glad there are objective reasons for them to dislike each other. Otherwise, Troy would just be an attractive twink, and there'd be no good reason for Lewin to hate him. He might even have to admit he enjoys his company.

Troy touches Lewin's still very clothed thigh. "What do you want?" he asks, somewhere between attentive and teasing. Mocking. Smirking. As if they're both in on a joke about them not being lovers and always have been. Cool. A big part of Lewin wants to roll away, make some excuse about needing to be at the station, and oops, he'd conveniently forgotten until it got awkward.

He settles for flinging an arm over his eyes and shrugging.

"Well, you clearly weren't into that," Troy says, actually sounding very reasonable. Like he's gearing up to Organize them both. "I mean, I don't need porn noises or anything, but a bit of enthusiasm is nice, or else I may as well just do it myself. So what is it? Are you into something weird? Is it embarrassing? Can you only enjoy it if there's a foot in your face, or something?"

Lewin drops his arm to glare at Troy. "No," he says. "And if that was your version of non-judgmental, it needs some work."

"Well…" Troy drops off his elbow, so they're both looking at the ceiling, not touching. "What do you like?"

Lewin shrugs again. This was a monumentally stupid idea. If Quentin and Jacob could just stop being so around and on top of each other, maybe Lewin wouldn't be feeling crazy enough to have tried something this dumb. "I don't know," he admits.

"You're not secretly straight, are you?" Troy asks. "Trying to fuck a young Republican can't be that traumatic."

"I'm not straight," Lewin tells the ceiling. "I like guys."

Troy suddenly sits up, turns, looks at Lewin with bright, wide eyes, and says, "this isn't your first time, is it?" Lewin laughs, short and sharp, and shakes his head no. "Fuck, good. Don't have hate sex as your first time. Christ."

"It's not," Lewin repeats. He slings his arm back over his eyes and says, "just. My last time wasn't great, and I don't really know what I like."

"Oh," Troy says. Then, in the careful way people talk to scared animals, he continues, "'not great', like…?"

"'Not great' like it wasn't great," Lewin tells him, heart beating so hard and fast he's not sure it comes out as condescending as he'd like. "It was awkward. Not 'not great' like I didn't want it and am traumatized. Why does everyone leap to that conclusion?"

Lewin peaks a glare and wishes he hadn't; Troy's look - concerned and cautious - is enough of an answer.

"Okay, well," he says, with the air of someone ignoring something that is someone else's problem. "What kind of porn do you like to watch? Maybe we could watch some and jerk each other off, or I'll blow you. Whatever."

Lewin's stomach twists. He shrugs again, caught up on the end of the statement rather than thinking through the implications of his answer.

Troy frowns at him. "It's something weird, isn't it?" he asks matter-of-factly. "It'll take a lot to surprise me, you know. My roommate likes girls with big tits dressed as cows, so. I'm pretty inoculated against weird porn."

Lewin scrunches his face at that image and thinks he'd probably have a lot of questions if he'd found this out at any other time. He just says, "Ew." Then shuts up, studying the ceiling and trying to think if there's anything that's ever made him feel… anything.

He shrugs again and says, "I don't really… porn doesn't really do it for me."

Troy gives him a skeptical look. "You've been watching the wrong kind of porn."

Lewin shrugs. "Maybe."

He doesn't think so.

Troy rolls his eyes, presumably at Lewin's lack of enthusiasm, before asking, clearly as a last resort, "Well, what do you jerk off to? What gets you off? Give me something to work with. Please."

Stopping his near-automatic shrug this time, Lewin bites his lip rather than admit he doesn't get himself off much, either. Of course, he does, but it's mostly quick and thoughtless when he does. Once in a blue moon, if he's got nothing to do or feels like treating himself or is suffering from a bout of insomnia, he'll strip off, lie back on his bed, close his eyes, and touch himself slowly, gently - luxuriating in it for an hour or more until finally coming. He likes the buildup, the anticipation, and that it's just for him. He feels comfortable and indulgent, and it's incredible, and then he comes, and it's over, and he might not do it again for months.

On those days, if he thinks about anything, it's nothing Troy would want to do.

(It's sharing a bed with someone. Being hugged from behind, a chin on his shoulder, scratchy stubble on his skin. Sometimes it's someone pushing him down on the bed, keeping him there, wanting him to stop moving. Other times he's face to face with someone, and they're nudging his nose with theirs, maybe kissing his eyelids when they fall closed.

It's someone trailing a line of kisses across his belly or just holding his hand.

In those fantasies, he might as well not have a dick.)

"You know what?" Lewin says, pushing himself up from Troy's bed and away from him. He pulls his shirt down, so it's stretched a little too far, looking around for his shoes. "This was a mistake. Sorry. I'll see you in class."

His shoes are under Troy's jacket. He grabs them, his own jacket, and leaves, not looking at Troy or listening to his half-indignant, half-concerned squawking.

Then he gets the fuck out of there.

⸻⸻•⸻⸻

Lewin enters the studio to the sound of Jonas laughing and at the end of what, from Dresden's body language, must have been a good long rant on the evils of the current administration. He's sad to have missed it. Could have saved up some of the best bits to use against Troy when he sees him in class tomorrow and needs to distract him.

"We're on the fence, clearly," Jonas is saying as Lewin slips into the booth quietly. He gets quick waves from Dresden and Jonas, smiles blandly at them, and sits in the back of the booth on their old, literally patchwork couch. "When we come back, we'll talk about the upcoming elections on campus, and it looks like we may have a special guest."

He presses play on an ad and swivels his chair towards Lewin, who says, "I'm not here to talk." And tips his head back against the couch back, closing his eyes.

There's a pause in which Lewin's sure Dresden and Jonas are making their surprise known to each other, but through which Lewin just ignores them, showing more restraint than he knew he had. Then, finally, Dresden says, "First time for everything, I guess." And Jonas adds, in a stage whisper, "Over/under on twenty minutes before he wrestles the mic from your hands?"

Lewin rolls his eyes. One of Olivia's crochet monstrosities has been flung over the back of the couch. Lewin flings it over himself instead as he lies down, his back to Jonas and Dresden, burying his face in the back of the couch with the crocket blanket over his face, so all the light and noise is muffled.

He hears Dresden ask, *sotto voce*, "Does he have an assignment due?" And Jonas murmur in the background, and then his eyes are closed, and he's pushing everything stressful away.

Lewin wakes to the couch dipping next to his head as someone slowly sits down, careful not to wake him. They're whispering to someone, saying, "doesn't he have a perfectly good bed at your place?" Something about the way they say it is less mocking than the words should be. There's nearly some concern in there.

"He panic naps," another voice replies at a normal volume. Jacob. Lewin can hear him over near the mics, rustling papers and moving things around. Dresden and Jonas must have finished and passed on to Studio B, leaving Studio A free for whatever Jacob's up to. Since he now realizes the person sitting next to him must be Quentin, Lewin's just hoping that what Jacob's up to has something to do with the station, not with having a date with the guy he's obsessed with.

Lewin rolls over onto his back, getting himself free of his crochet swaddling with minimal embarrassing writhing and turning his head to glare at Jacob. "I am not panic napping," he tells them. Mostly Jacob, who already has eyebrows raised to prepare for this very argument. "I am resetting my brain so I can think. People in Europe sleep in the middle of the day *every day*. We're the weird ones who don't. Society would be better if we all just agreed that our brains work better if we sleep during the hot part of the day. Don't give me that look, *Jacob*."

Jacob is laughing at him. He glances at Quentin and seems to catch on him, eyes sparkling as he subtly pulls a series of micro-expressions, with Quentin letting out a chuckle.

"Ugh," Lewin says, looking between them in exasperation and ignoring the knot in his stomach. "You two have been dating for, what, a month? Fuck off with this talking-without-words shit. Get a room."

Jacob laughs, missing the look Quentin gives Lewin, the one that Lewin isn't sure how to interpret but makes him feel like he's done something wrong. Maybe he has. It's not fair to be so obvious about this when he gave Quentin his blessing to make Jacob disgustingly happy.

Which he is, as far as Lewin can tell. Which is great. It's just, sharing a wall with Jacob has been a lot since they got together.

"We did," Quentin tells him, gesturing around. He leans forward and pulls out a notebook, a pen and a book that looks like something even Jacob would fall asleep over. "Is there a reason why you didn't?"

Lewin pretends he didn't hear that. Instead, he squints at Quentin's notes, trying to read his spidery handwriting. "Notes from class?" he asks.

"Notes for a piece I'm writing about *this* guy," Quentin replies, letting Lewin's ignored question go and showing him the front of the book. Lewin has never heard of the guy the book mentions.

"For the Herald?" The Herald is the school paper, and Lewin knows Quentin is constantly working on something for it and is on the editing staff. He doesn't think he's ever picked up a copy himself except the two big stories it'd run on his Friday night shows and his, Jonas and Jacob's takeover of the station.

"For the Washington Post," Quentin responds, voice dry. Jacob snorts.

"Lewin, are you up for helping me record some ads?" Jacob asks. He invitingly pats the other swivel chair opposite him. "We could get ahead of schedule…"

"You say that like it's an enticement," Lewin informs him. He turns to Quentin. "Is his dirty talk this bad in bed, too?"

Quentin laughs, full-throated, eyes crinkled at the edges as they dance between Jacob and Lewin. Jacob has gone bright red even as he rolls his eyes and turns back to the audio equipment in front of him.

"I'll take that as a no," Jacob says.

"Quentin can record them with you," Lewin tells him. "Give the listeners the full newly-wed dynamic. They'll eat it up. I'm not quite done with my panic nap."

He lies back, hair brushing Quentin's thigh. He repeats every word he's said in this conversation to himself and tells himself: *stop. flirting. idiot.*

"Quentin cannot," Quentin says, in a tone that's near singsong. Talking in the third person about yourself should be an instant turn-off. Lewin feels about how Jacob looks regarding it, though: fond, and confused about it. "I'm, uh… not exactly advertising… This." He gestures mostly between him and Jacob, but a little around the room.

Lewin tilts his head back so he can see all of Quentin's face, seeing the downturn to his lips and the quick, uncertain glance he throws Jacob, then Lewin. "Are you not out?" Lewin asks. "Shit, no judgment, Quentin, but tell people that, please. It's not like I go around announcing all the people I know are queer, but if you're not out, I don't want to fuck things up for you."

Quentin shakes his head. Jacob, either deciding he's not getting done what needs to be while this conversation is happening or wanting to be a supportive boyfriend, gets up and shoves Lewin's feet out of the way, so he has room to sit with the two on the couch. He twists a little, so he's watching Quentin, arm flung over the back so his fingers brush Quentin's shoulder. Finally, he picks up Lewin's feet by the ankles and pulls them back onto his lap.

"I'm out to the people who matter," Quentin says. "My mom and family and all my friends, here. I just… don't advertise it. It's not a big deal, and if it gets out, it gets out, but occasionally I still get a reporter to come want to talk to me about some dumb story or another and I'd rather not add fuel to the fire."

Lewin frowns, noting Jacob's supportive little smile and Quentin's grateful one.

"Reporters?" Lewin says. "Why do you get reporters talking to you?"

Jacob laughs, telling Quentin, "I told you he had no idea."

Quentin, looking a little perplexed and a little pleased, says, "Do you not use Google?"

"What?" Lewin asks, automatic. "Who Googles people they know in real life?"

Quentin laughs, Jacob, joining in a second later. "Who doesn't, as far as I'm concerned," Quentin tells him. Then, "my mom's an actress. And the, uh, my two possible biological fathers are famous, too. It's calmed down, recently, since none of them have done anything that new and exciting for a while, but during my first degree, it got really bad for a while when-"

"Your *first* degree?" Lewin asks, voice going up. "What the fuck? This is a prank, right? That was way too many ridiculous things all at once."

Quentin sends Jacob an amused look and Jacob laughs, saying, "Hey, I told you. He's oblivious."

"Don't give me that shit," Lewin tells him, still swaddled enough in his crochet cocoon he can't literally point a finger at him, so he does the best he can with his eyes, instead. "He was a guest on your show; of course, you Googled him."

"I'm not pranking you," Quentin assures him. He's got this soft, slightly mocking look around his eyes that Lewin doesn't hate, but does hate how much he doesn't hate it. "Jacob met me through Dresden. We're in the same Human Rights workshop. I'm studying Law."

Lewin looks between Quentin and Jacob, disadvantaged from his horizontal position in the effort he's making to figure out if Quentin is for real, but concluding that he… probably is, actually. Jacob loves an overachiever.

"How old are you?" Lewin asks. "Please tell me Jacob is your toy boy."

Quentin laughs, shaking his head. "No, I'm twenty."

"Which means you were, what, fourteen when you went to college?"

Quentin pulls a face, shaking his head. "No," he says, "I was fourteen when I first applied to Law Schools."

"Oh Christ, Jacob, you found someone even more…" Lewin frees an arm so he can gesture up and down Jacob's too-tall body. "Jacob, than you."

Jacob and Quentin laugh, looking equally delighted by how perplexed and thrown for a loop Lewin feels. Jacob puts a big hand over Lewin's ankle and squeezes in warning, saying, "Hey, I know you must mean that as a compliment, but you really need to work on your tone."

Lewin makes a sound of disgust, watching as Quentin straightens his face and buries himself in his book, quickly looking engrossed. Overachiever.

"Didn't you have ads to record?" Lewin asks Jacob, poking him in the belly with his socked toe. "Stop slacking."

Jacob smiles indulgently, pushing himself up and Lewin's feet to the floor only incidentally. "Going to help me, then?" Jacob asks, stretching. Lewin looks away, eyes catching on the furrow in Quentin's brow instead.

He's thinking of saying, "Nah, too comfy." And is opening his mouth to say just that when Quentin makes a noise between a sigh and a curious "hm", twisting in his seat to get more comfortable. He ends up with one of his legs tucked up under him, thigh brushing against Lewin's hair, free arm over the couch above him. Like he's comfortable here, in Lewin's space, and Lewin both loves and hates how comfortable he feels in Quentin's space.

He looks at Jacob, feeling guilt pool in his stomach like vinegar - burning and acidic.

Jacob is watching him, looking fond. He does flick a glance between Lewin and Quentin - looks like he's thinking - but he's not suspicious. Or mad. *Why would he be?* Lewin supposes. It's only Lewin who thinks of being comfortable in someone's space as this big of a deal.

"Sure," Lewin says. He holds a hand up towards Jacob. "Pull me up. Let's get this ad show on the road."